leapfrog

Rhyme
Time

Miss Lupin's Motorbike

First published in 2008 by
Franklin Watts
338 Euston Road
London
NW1 3BH

Franklin Watts Australia
Level 17/207 Kent Street
Sydney
NSW 2000

Text © Sue Graves 2008
Illustration © Roger Fereday 2008

JS

A CIP catalogue record for this book is available
from the British Library.

ISBN 978 0 7496 7945 3 (hbk)
ISBN 978 0 7496 7957 6 (pbk)

Series Editor: Jackie Hamley
Series Advisor: Dr Barrie Wade
Series Designer: Peter Scoulding

Printed in China

Franklin Watts is a division of
Hachette Children's Books,
an Hachette Livre UK company.

Miss Lupin's Motorbike

by Sue Graves

Illustrated by Roger Fereday

FRANKLIN WATTS
LONDON•SYDNEY

Miss Lupin got a motorbike
from everyone at school.

It was what she'd always wanted. It made her feel quite cool!

The motorbike was shiny.
It had stripes of red
and white.

But when she tried
to ride it ...

... it gave her such a fright!

The motorbike sped up
the road.

It roared around the town.

It raced right up
the high street ...

12

... and then it
raced back down.

It sped around the
farmyard, and gave
the cows a scare.

It tore straight through
the meadow, and splashed
mud everywhere!

"Stop! Stop!" cried Jake
the policeman.

18

"Stop! Stop!" everyone cried.

But Miss Lupin couldn't slow down, no matter how she tried.

21

Miss Lupin rode across the moor, but then she got an itch.

The bike span as she
let it go ...

... then landed in a ditch!

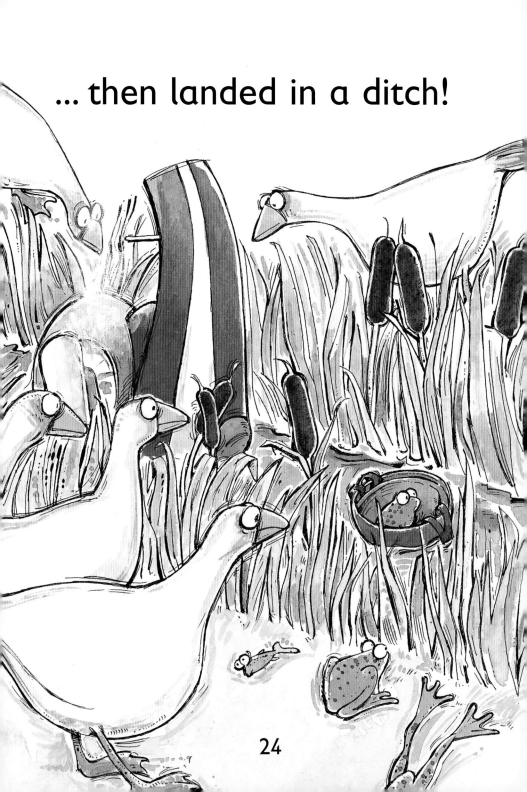

Everybody ran to help her.
"Why didn't you stop?"
asked Jake.

Miss Lupin tried to smile and said, "I couldn't find the brake."

So Miss Lupin's had
some lessons.

She has found out how
to stop.

And now she's passed her safety test, back on her bike she'll hop!

TEST CENTRE

Leapfrog Rhyme Time has been specially designed to fit the requirements of the Literacy Framework. It offers real books for beginner readers by top authors and illustrators. There are 27 Leapfrog Rhyme Time stories to choose from:

RHYME TIME

Mr Spotty's Potty
ISBN 978 0 7496 3831 3

Eight Enormous Elephants
ISBN 978 0 7496 4634 9

Freddie's Fears
ISBN 978 0 7496 4382 9

Squeaky Clean
ISBN 978 0 7496 6805 1

Craig's Crocodile
ISBN 978 0 7496 6806 8

Felicity Floss: Tooth Fairy
ISBN 978 0 7496 6807 5

Captain Cool
ISBN 978 0 7496 6808 2

Monster Cake
ISBN 978 0 7496 6809 9

The Super Trolley Ride
ISBN 978 0 7496 6810 5

The Royal Jumble Sale
ISBN 978 0 7496 6811 2

But, Mum!
ISBN 978 0 7496 6812 9

Dan's Gran's Goat
ISBN 978 0 7496 6814 3

Lighthouse Mouse
ISBN 978 0 7496 6815 0

Big Bad Bart
ISBN 978 0 7496 6816 7

Ron's Race
ISBN 978 0 7496 6817 4

Woolly the Bully
ISBN 978 0 7496 7098 6*
ISBN 978 0 7496 7790 9

Boris the Spider
ISBN 978 0 7496 7099 3*
ISBN 978 0 7496 7791 6

Miss Polly's Seaside Brolly
ISBN 978 0 7496 7100 6*
ISBN 978 0 7496 7792 3

Juggling Joe
ISBN 978 0 7496 7103 7*
ISBN 978 0 7496 7795 4

What a Frog!
ISBN 978 0 7496 7102 0*
ISBN 978 0 7496 7794 7

The Lonely Pirate
ISBN 978 0 7496 7101 3*
ISBN 978 0 7496 7793 0

I Wish!
ISBN 978 0 7496 7940 8*
ISBN 978 0 7496 7952 1

Raindrop Bill
ISBN 978 0 7496 7941 5*
ISBN 978 0 7496 7953 8

Sir Otto
ISBN 978 0 7496 7942 2*
ISBN 978 0 7496 7954 5

Queen Rosie
ISBN 978 0 7496 7943 9*
ISBN 978 0 7496 7955 2

Giraffe's Good Game
ISBN 978 0 7496 7944 6*
ISBN 978 0 7496 7956 9

Miss Lupin's Motorbike
ISBN 978 0 7496 7945 3*
ISBN 978 0 7496 7957 6

Look out for Leapfrog
FAIRY TALES

Cinderella
ISBN 978 0 7496 4228 0

The Three Little Pigs
ISBN 978 0 7496 4227 3

Jack and the Beanstalk
ISBN 978 0 7496 4229 7

The Three Billy Goats Gruff
ISBN 978 0 7496 4226 6

Goldilocks and the Three Bears
ISBN 978 0 7496 4225 9

Little Red Riding Hood
ISBN 978 0 7496 4224 2

Rapunzel
ISBN 978 0 7496 6159 5

Snow White
ISBN 978 0 7496 6161 8

The Emperor's New Clothes
ISBN 978 0 7496 6163 2

The Pied Piper of Hamelin
ISBN 978 0 7496 6164 9

Hansel and Gretel
ISBN 978 0 7496 6162 5

The Sleeping Beauty
ISBN 978 0 7496 6160 1

Rumpelstiltskin
ISBN 978 0 7496 6165 6

The Ugly Duckling
ISBN 978 0 7496 6166 3

Puss in Boots
ISBN 978 0 7496 6167 0

The Frog Prince
ISBN 978 0 7496 6168 7

The Princess and the Pea
ISBN 978 0 7496 6169 4

Dick Whittington
ISBN 978 0 7496 6170 0

The Elves and the Shoemaker
ISBN 978 0 7496 6581 4

The Little Match Girl
ISBN 978 0 7496 6582 1

The Little Mermaid
ISBN 978 0 7496 6583 8

The Little Red Hen
ISBN 978 0 7496 6585 2

The Nightingale
ISBN 978 0 7496 6586 9

Thumbelina
ISBN 978 0 7496 6587 6

Other Leapfrog titles also available.